Augustus et son Sourire

Augustus and his Smile

This book is TalkingPEN™ enabled.

You can hear the text narrated on any page in English and another language.
1.   Touch the **arrow** button below with TalkingPEN to start.
2.   Touch the **English** or **language** button to select your language.
3.   Touch the top corner of any page to hear the text narrated.
     Switch language at any time by clicking the *'mode'* button on TalkingPEN.
4.   TalkingPEN can hold lots of languages for this title. To select a new
     language touch the **arrow** and then the **language** button again.
     Repeat this until you reach the language you want. Then follow step 2.
5.   To order new languages please go to www.talkingpen.co.uk

English   language

Text and Illustrations copyright © Catherine Rayner 2006
Catherine Raynor has asserted her right to be identified as the author and
illustrator of this work under the Copyright, Designs and Patents Act, 1988
Dual language copyright © Mantra Lingua 2008

Mantra Lingua
303 Ballards Lnae, London N12 8NP
www.mantralingua.com
www.talkingpen.co.uk

First published in UK
This edition published 2008
by Little Tiger Press 2006

Audio copyright ©
Mantra Lingua 2008

Thank you, Mum, Brian and Colin - C R

Augustus et son Sourire

Augustus and his Smile

Catherine Rayner

French translation by
Annie Arnold

mantra lingua

Augustus le tigre était triste.
Il avait perdu son sourire.

Augustus the tiger was sad.
He had lost his smile.

Alors il fit un ENORME étirement de tigre et partit pour le trouver.

So he did a HUGE tigery stretch and set off to find it.

D'abord il rampa sous des buissons. Il trouva un petit scarabée brillant, mais il ne pouvait pas voir son sourire.

First he crept under a cluster of bushes. He found a small, shiny beetle, but he couldn't see his smile.

Then he climbed to the tops of the tallest trees.
He found birds that chirped and called,
but he couldn't find his smile.

Puis il grimpa tout en haut des plus grands arbres.
Il trouva des oiseaux qui gazouillaient et appelaient,
mais il ne pouvait pas trouver son sourire.

De plus en plus loin Augustus cherchait.
Il grimpa aux cimes des plus hautes montagnes là où les
nuages de neige tourbillonnaient faisant des dessins gelés
dans l'air glacial.

Further and further Augustus searched.
He scaled the crests of the highest mountains where the snow
clouds swirled, making frost patterns in the freezing air.

Il nagea au fond des océans profonds et s'éclaboussa et pataugea parmi des bancs de minuscules poissons brillants.

He swam to the bottom of the deepest oceans and splished and splashed with shoals of tiny, shiny fish.

Il caracola et parada à travers le plus grand désert, faisant
des formes avec les ombres du soleil. Augustus marcha à
pas feutrés de plus en plus loin
      à travers les sables mouvants
            jusqu'à …

He pranced and paraded through
the largest desert, making
shadow shapes in the sun.
Augustus padded further
   and further
      through shifting sand
        until …

... pitter patter

pitter patter

drip

drop

plop!

… flac floc

flac floc

flac

floc

plouf !

Augustus dansa
et courut
alors que les gouttes
rebondissaient
et s'envolaient.

Augustus danced
and raced
as raindrops bounced
and flew.

Il s'éclaboussa dans les flaques, de plus en plus grandes et profondes.
Il courut vers une énorme flaque bleue argentée et a vu …

He splashed through puddles, bigger and deeper.
He raced towards a huge silver-blue puddle
and saw …

… là sous son nez
          … son sourire !

… there under his nose
          … his smile!

Et Augustus réalisa que son sourire serait là chaque fois qu'il serait heureux.
Il n'avait qu'à nager avec les poissons ou danser dans les flaques, ou grimper aux montagnes et regarder le monde - parce que la joie était partout autour de lui.

Augustus était si heureux qu'il sauta et gambada …

And Augustus realised that his smile would be there, whenever he was happy.

He only had to swim with the fish or dance in the puddles, or climb the mountains and look at the world – for happiness was everywhere around him.

Augustus was so pleased that
he hopped
and skipped …

… et s'en alla en bondissant,
souriant.

… and jumped away,
smiling.